Please help the bunnies of Moonglow Meadow!

Our brave and loyal friend, Arrow, has travelled far from our world to protect the magic key that keeps our kingdom safe from the dark rabbits. Arrow is very far from home and will need your help.

Could you be his friend?

This magic bunny might be hard to spot as he is very small and often appears in different fluffy bunny disguises – but you can recognize him by the rainbow twinkle in his eyes.

 your help!

Strike
Leader of Moonglow Meadow

Sue Bentley's books for children often include animals, fairies and magic. She lives in Northampton in a house surrounded by a hedge so she can pretend she's in the middle of the countryside. She loves reading and going to the cinema, and writes while watching the birds on the feeders outside her window and eating chocolate. Sue was brought up surrounded by small animals and loved them all – especially her gentle pet rabbits whose fur smelled so sweetly of rain and grass.

Sue Bentley

Magic Bunny

Holiday Dreams

Illustrated by Angela Swan

PUFFIN

To Daisy, cute and fluffy, lop-eared childhood friend

PUFFIN BOOKS

Published by the Penguin Group
Penguin Books Ltd, 80 Strand, London WC2R 0RL, England
Penguin Group (USA) Inc., 375 Hudson Street, New York, New York 10014, USA
Penguin Group (Canada), 90 Eglinton Avenue East, Suite 700, Toronto, Ontario, Canada M4P 2Y3
(a division of Pearson Penguin Canada Inc.)
Penguin Ireland, 25 St Stephen's Green, Dublin 2, Ireland (a division of Penguin Books Ltd)
Penguin Group (Australia), 250 Camberwell Road, Camberwell, Victoria 3124, Australia
(a division of Pearson Australia Group Pty Ltd)
Penguin Books India Pvt Ltd, 11 Community Centre, Panchsheel Park, New Delhi – 110 017, India
Penguin Group (NZ), 67 Apollo Drive, Rosedale, North Shore 0632, New Zealand
(a division of Pearson New Zealand Ltd)
Penguin Books (South Africa) (Pty) Ltd, 24 Sturdee Avenue, Rosebank,
Johannesburg 2196, South Africa

Penguin Books Ltd, Registered Offices: 80 Strand, London WC2R 0RL, England

puffinbooks.com

First published 2010
004

Text copyright © Sue Bentley, 2010
Illustrations copyright © Angela Swan, 2010
All rights reserved

The moral right of the author and illustrator has been asserted

Set in Bembo
Made and printed in England by Clays Ltd, St Ives plc

British Library Cataloguing in Publication Data
A CIP catalogue record for this book is available from the British Library

ISBN: 978-0-141-33242-0

www.greenpenguin.co.uk

MIX
Paper from
responsible sources
FSC™ C018179
www.fsc.org

Penguin Books is committed to a sustainable
future for our business, our readers and our planet.
This book is made from Forest Stewardship
Council™ certified paper.

ALWAYS LEARNING   **PEARSON**

Prologue

Arrow looked round at Moonglow Meadow. Many of his fellow magic rabbits were hopping about on the dry patchy ground and others were nibbling wilted plants. He had returned just in time.

The tiny gold key he wore on a chain round his neck glowed brightly and a cloud of crystal dust rose into the air. It sprinkled down gently and a lush carpet of fresh grass and brightly coloured wild flowers appeared and spread until it covered the whole meadow.

The hungry rabbits began to eat. Some of the younger ones rolled over and over, getting the scent of the dewy grass on their fur.

An older rabbit hopped towards Arrow. He had a dark grey muzzle and wore a wise expression.

'Strike!' Arrow bowed his head in greeting before the leader of the warren.

'It is good to see you again, Arrow,' Strike said in a deep velvety voice. 'We chose well when we made you keeper of our magic key.'

Arrow felt a surge of pride at the leader's praise. He knew that he would guard the key with his life.

Suddenly, there was a commotion at the far side of Moonglow Meadow and Arrow saw a group of rabbits rushing towards them.

'The-the dark rabbits are coming!' one of them squealed, wide-eyed with panic.

Arrow flattened his silver-tipped ears nervously. The dark rabbits lived nearby in a deep gulley. The land had become so dry that nothing grew there and they were hungry, but the dark rabbits had refused Strike's invitation to live with them in Moonglow Meadow.

'They are coming to steal our magic key,' Strike rumbled, 'and use it to make their gulley green and beautiful again.'

'But without the key's power, Moonglow Meadow will become a desert!' Arrow gasped.

'That is why you must go to the Otherworld once more,' Strike said gravely. 'Hide there so the dark rabbits cannot find the key!'

Arrow felt very young and scared, but he knew the warren was relying on him. 'I will do it!'

Strike gave a soft but piercing cry.

Every rabbit in the warren came speeding towards them and formed a circle around Arrow. Suddenly, the golden key hanging from Arrow's neck glowed very brightly.

The light slowly faded and where the pure white-and-silver magic rabbit had been now stood a tiny pale-coffee-coloured bunny with fluffy fur and huge brown eyes that twinkled with tiny rainbows.

'Go now! Use this disguise,' Strike said. 'Only return when Moonglow Meadow needs more of the key's magic. And watch out for the dark rabbits!'

Arrow held up his tiny fluffy head. 'I will!'

Thud. Thud. Thud. The rabbits began thumping their feet in time. Arrow felt the magic building and a cloud of crystal dust shimmered around him as Moonglow Meadow grew fainter and fainter . . .

Chapter
ONE

Becky Hodge woke early with a feeling of excitement. 'Yay! It's half-term!' she cried, thinking of all the things she could do with her friends – tennis, swimming, maybe even riding. She flung back the duvet, almost falling out of bed in her eagerness to get up.

A shaft of early morning sunlight streamed into the darkened room through a heart-shaped hole in the wooden shutters. Becky frowned in puzzlement.

Wooden shutters? Her bedroom didn't have . . .

And then she remembered where she was. 'Foxglove Farm!'

Becky was staying at her aunt and uncle's farm while her mum and Aunty Katy were away on a business course. They ran classes in country crafts and knitting.

Even though it was a bit strange being at the farm with only Uncle Den and her cousin Leon, who played computer games all day, at least there was more to do on the farm than at her house. Her dad was at home working on an important assignment for his job and needed peace and quiet – and that was not how Becky wanted to spend her half-term!

'See if you can't drag Leon away from his computer for an hour or two,' Dad had said as he kissed her goodbye last night. 'If you can't, no one can!'

Becky grinned to herself as she went to the bedroom shutters. Dad was always teasing her about being too enthusiastic and not taking 'no' for an answer.

She stood looking out at the view of the farmyard with its huge barns and fields full of corn and vegetables.

There was the faint outline of a village far away in the distance; beyond that, all she could see were thick woods and the green slopes of rolling hills.

Becky sighed as she turned away from the window. The farm was miles from any other people. She had no choice but to make the best of things.

As she dressed in jeans and a T-shirt, she tried hard to think of something Leon might like doing besides playing computer games. Football! All boys liked that, didn't they? Maybe she could persuade him to come outside and play.

She was pulling on her trainers when there was a knock at the door.

'Come in!' Becky called.

Leon stuck his head round the door. He had sandy hair that flopped over his forehead and serious blue eyes. At twelve years old, he was three years older than Becky.

'Hi, Leon! Do you fancy having a kickabout with a football later? I'm pretty good at sports. Look!' Becky shuffled her feet encouragingly as if she was dribbling a ball. But in her eagerness she caught the toe of her trainer on the rug and almost tripped up.

Leon looked at her curiously. 'Er, sorry, I can't. I've got some stuff to finish.'

'Oh . . . OK then. Well, when you've finished, maybe we can do something together?' Becky tried again. 'How about tennis or cricket? Or you could show me around those woods —'

'Maybe later.' Leon edged out of the doorway and called from the landing,

'I only came to tell you that breakfast's ready!'

Becky tried to ignore a growing feeling of dismay as she followed her cousin downstairs. Maybe Leon didn't like hanging around with younger kids. Whenever Becky was here, he always stayed in his room.

Uncle Den sat at the kitchen table drinking tea and reading a farming magazine. He looked up and smiled as Becky came in. 'Hello, love. Did you sleep well?'

'Yes, thanks.' Becky returned his smile as she sat down next to Leon, who was staring into space as if he was deep in thought.

'This is Mrs Kelly.' Her uncle nodded towards a small round figure bustling about at the stove. He explained that she'd be doing the cooking and housekeeping while Becky's aunt was away.

'Hello, Mrs Kelly,' Becky said cheerfully.

'Good morning.' Mrs Kelly smiled back at Becky, but only briefly. Her grey hair was pinned into a neat bun and a spotless

apron covered her blue flowered dress.
She placed a steaming dish of eggs, bacon,
beans and sausages on the table, followed
by a rack of toast.

'There you are. Help yourselves.'

Becky could feel her tummy rumbling
at the sight of the feast in front of her.
She began loading her plate.

While they all ate, the housekeeper
banged about, washing pots and pans at
the speed of light. She then strode into
the utility room next to the kitchen.
Becky heard a whooshing sound as the
washing machine went into action.

'I'll be giving those bedsheets a good
flap outside in the fresh air,' Mrs Kelly
said loudly, to no one in particular.
'I don't hold with those new-fangled
tumble-dryers and such.'

What's the big deal? Becky wondered. *Mum tumble-drys our washing – doesn't everyone?*

Becky finished everything on her plate. She was just enjoying some toast with real butter and marmalade, when Leon stood up and asked to be excused from the table. 'It's OK, isn't it, Dad? I've got something really important to do.'

'All right, off you go. But I don't want you shut away upstairs for hours on end while Becky's staying with us,' his father said. 'I'm relying on you to entertain our guest.'

'Yeah, course I will. Just as soon as I finish this!' Leon said over his shoulder, already rushing out.

Becky heard him clattering upstairs and then slamming his bedroom door.

Uncle Den shook his head slowly as he turned to Becky. 'Leon writes a column for an online magazine – or "'zine", as he calls it. He takes it very seriously. Are you keen on computers, love?'

'They're OK. But I get bored sitting down all the time,' Becky replied. 'I usually prefer being outside and doing stuff.'

'An action girl, eh? Sounds like you'll be good for Leon!'

Becky smiled, hoping he was right. But things didn't look too promising. Leon hadn't shown much interest in spending any time with her so far.

Uncle Den began reading the adverts page. A kitchen clock ticked loudly in the silence.

Becky finished her toast. She leaned

forward and propped her chin on one
hand, wondering what she might do
next. *Is it worth going upstairs and trying to
persuade Leon to come exploring with me or
shall I just go on my own?*

'We'll be having no elbows on the
table, young lady, if you please!' A stern
voice spoke close to her ear as Mrs Kelly
reached for Becky's empty plate.

Becky almost jumped out of her skin.
'Um . . . sorry.'

She blushed as she quickly leaned back and put her hands in her lap. No one minded about stuff like that at home.

Uncle Den put down his magazine and stood up. 'Don't mind Mrs Kelly. She has very high standards. But her bark's a lot worse than her bite,' he said, winking at her. 'Well – I've a rabbit problem to see about. The little devils have been playing havoc with my crops and I've got to take some serious action. You and Leon have a good day. If you need anything, just ask Mrs Kelly.'

'OK. See you later,' Becky said.

Mrs Kelly was now sliding a floor mop under the table. As it almost whisked across her trainers, Becky leapt up out of her chair and headed into the back garden. The housekeeper was seriously scary.

It had been raining earlier, but the sun was shining now and everything smelled fresh. Becky made her way round the side of the house. One of the farm workers was driving a tractor across the farmyard and another was coming out of the barn. They smiled and waved at her so Becky waved back.

She spotted a gate that led into a field with a duck pond. She went through and wandered over the damp grass.

There were a number of wild rabbits hopping about in the next field, their white cottontails flashing.

'Watch out! Uncle Den will be after you if you get into his crops!' she warned them.

Suddenly, there was a bright flash and a shower of crystal dust drifted towards her in a twinkling cloud.

'Oh!' Becky narrowed her eyes, trying to peer through it. As the dust slowly cleared, she spotted a fluffy pale-coffee-coloured bunny on the grass right in front of her.

'Can you help me, please?' it asked in a scared little voice.

Chapter
TWO

Becky's jaw dropped and she stared at
the cute little bunny in total amazement.
Perhaps it was someone's pet. She didn't
know a lot about pet bunnies, but she was
pretty sure that they couldn't talk.

She laughed at herself. Just because
Leon wouldn't talk to her, it didn't mean
a rabbit would!

The pale brown bunny's little pink nose

twitched nervously and it looked up at
her with huge eyes like chocolate drops.

Becky edged closer and slowly bent
down, trying not to frighten it.

'Hello. Aren't you sweet?' she crooned.
'You don't seem all that scared of me. Do
you want to make friends?'

'Yes. I would like that very much,' the
bunny said in a trembly little voice.

'Whoa!' Becky gasped in shock. She

lost her balance and sat down hard on the damp grass. 'You . . . you really *can* talk!'

'Yes. All of my warren can talk. I am Arrow, guardian of Moonglow Meadow,' the cute bunny told her, his long floppy ears lifting proudly. 'What is your name?'

'Um . . . Rebecca. Rebecca Hodge. But everyone calls me Becky. This is my uncle's farm. I'm staying here while my mum and aunt are away on a course.' She noticed that Arrow's deep brown eyes seemed to be glimmering with tiny rainbows.

The bunny bowed his head. 'I am honoured to meet you, Becky.'

'Me too.' Becky moved on to her knees, wondering if she should curtsy or something, but she finally settled for just dipping her chin. 'Is Moonglow Meadow another one of Uncle Den's fields?'

'No. It is far from here. In another world,' Arrow explained. As he lifted his chin, something round his neck twinkled. Becky saw that he wore a fine gold chain with a key hanging from it.

'What's that?' she asked him.

'The magic key, which I must keep safe from the fierce dark rabbits. Their land is dry and stony and they are hungry, but they refuse to share our land with us. They want to steal the key and use it to make only their land lush and green. But if they do this, Moonglow Meadow will become a desert.'

'Oh no! That would be terrible!' Becky exclaimed.

'Yes. I will not let it happen!' A determined look crossed Arrow's fluffy face. 'That is why I agreed to come here all by myself.'

Becky was still having trouble taking all this in, but fascination was starting to take over from shock. Arrow's world sounded so strange and magical.

She smiled warmly at him. 'You're very brave for such a tiny bunny.'

Arrow raised himself onto his back legs and flicked his tail mischievously.

'I am not so small. Please stay back!' he ordered.

Becky felt a weird warm prickling sensation down her spine as the key round Arrow's neck began flashing and a cloud of twinkling crystal dust swirled around him. When it cleared Becky saw that the little bunny had gone and in his place was the most stunning rabbit she had ever seen. It was as big as a large cat and had silky white fur, flecked with silver. The tips of its ears twinkled with what looked like molten silver, and big jewel-bright rainbows flashed from its eyes.

Becky gasped in amazement. She'd never seen anything so majestic or so beautiful.

'Arrow?' she gulped.

'Yes, Becky. It is still me,' Arrow said in a smooth voice.

Before she had got used to seeing him in his true form, there was a final flash of light from his key and Arrow reappeared as a pale-coffee-coloured bunny.

'Wow! That's a cool disguise!' Becky exclaimed.

Arrow twitched his nose nervously. 'I am afraid the dark rabbits will see through it if they catch up with me. I must find a place to hide, and quickly.'

Becky's heart went out to the brave little bunny. She wanted to do all she could to help him. 'You can live in my bedroom. Wait until I tell my cousin Leon about you. He might even talk to me then and –'

'No, I am sorry, Becky, my mission is secret. You can tell no one. Please promise me,' the magic bunny asked anxiously.

Becky felt a little bit disappointed. She had been hoping that Leon would want to spend more time with her if he saw that she had a magical new friend. But she also felt proud that Arrow was prepared to trust her with such an important secret.

'OK then, I promise,' she agreed. 'I'll smuggle you into the farmhouse. No one's going to notice. Mrs Kelly will be too busy doing housework and Leon's on his computer. He doesn't even seem that bothered about me being here.'

Arrow dipped his head gratefully. 'I would like to live with you very much. Thank you, Becky.'

'You're welcome!' Becky scooted towards him on her knees and reached out her cupped hands. Arrow jumped straight into them.

She felt him snuggle up against her as she stood up. A happy feeling glowed inside Becky as she thought about having a secret friend all to herself for this week – especially such an amazing one as Arrow!

Chapter
THREE

Becky cradled Arrow close as she walked
back across the field. At the gate that
opened on to the farmyard, she paused.

'We'll sneak in through the back door.
I don't particularly want to bump into
Mrs Kelly,' she said to Arrow. 'Uh-oh!' she
whispered, quickly ducking behind the
gate as the farmhouse door opened and
the housekeeper appeared.

Becky didn't want to have to answer awkward questions if she was caught with Arrow, so she crouched out of sight until Mrs Kelly went off towards the henhouse.

'Phew! That was close!' Becky slipped through the gate and, cuddling Arrow close, sprinted across the yard and slipped round to the back of the farmhouse.

She looked down at her new friend as she walked across the lawn. Arrow was so cute. He had stretched up to lie full-length against her chest, and his eyes were closed contentedly as she stroked his pale fur. It was the softest thing she had ever touched.

'Oh!' Becky felt something very big and wet flap against her face.

A bedsheet! She hadn't been looking where she was going and had stumbled

into a line of clean washing. A gust of
wind made a corner of the sheet flick
over Becky's shoulder with a cracking
sound.

Arrow gave a squeal of terror and tried
to leap out of her arms.

'It's OK, Arrow, it's only a sheet!'

But the terrified magic bunny didn't
seem to be listening. He kicked out with
his back legs, accidentally scratching
Becky's chest through her T-shirt.

Becky winced at the stinging soreness, but she made herself ignore it as she struggled to keep hold of her tiny friend without squeezing him too hard. She was worried that he'd hurt himself if he jumped to the ground from such a height. But her trainers slipped on the damp grass and Becky felt herself tumbling forward. Stretching out one hand, she grabbed at the nearest sheet to save herself.

Snap! Snap! Snap! Clothespegs pinged off the line as Becky collapsed into a heap of wet washing.

'Ooof!' She managed to twist round and land on her back, keeping Arrow safe in her cupped hands. Becky lay there for a moment, too stunned to move. She could feel Arrow's rapid heartbeat against her palm.

'Are you OK?' Becky asked him
worriedly.

'I am fine. You saved me. Thank you!'
Arrow moved up to nudge her chin
gently with his little wet nose.

Relief washed through Becky. She'd
only had Arrow for a short time, but she
already loved her magical friend to bits
and couldn't bear to think of him being
hurt.

She struggled to get free of the clinging
damp material.

'Oh!' As Becky finally managed to
stand up, the stinging came back. Now
that the excitement was over, the claw
marks Arrow had made in his panic were
starting to smart horribly.

Arrow laid his ears flat with concern.
'You are hurt, Becky. Let me help you!'

Becky saw Arrow's key start to pulse
with light and felt a warm prickling
sensation down her spine. He twitched
his little pink nose and a fountain of
crystal dust appeared, shimmering with
a thousand tiny rainbows.

To Becky's amazement, the magical
dust spread all over the front of her
T-shirt, before seeming to sink into it and
disappear. The scratch marks turned cold

and then stopped hurting completely as if they'd never been there at all.

When Becky peered down inside her T-shirt to check, there wasn't a single mark to be seen.

'Cool! Thanks, Arrow. I'm fine now. Come on. Let's get you inside before –'

'My washing!' boomed a furious voice. 'What have you done, you dreadful girl?'

Becky froze in terror. She slowly turned to see Mrs Kelly standing in the kitchen doorway. She was staring at Becky's feet.

Becky looked down too, horrified to see that she was standing on a heap of trampled muddy sheets. She had been so worried about Arrow that she hadn't given a thought to the washing.

'I am in so much trouble!' Becky

groaned, expecting a double telling-off.
She was still holding the fluffy bunny,
who was now tucked safely under one
arm. Mrs Kelly seemed the sort who
wouldn't allow animals into the house.

'Just look at those sheets!' The
housekeeper marched into the garden
with a face like thunder. Becky leapt
backwards in alarm, leaving another
perfect muddy trainer print on a clean bit
of sheet.

'It was an . . . um . . . accident,' she
burbled lamely. 'Sorry.'

'A likely story!' Mrs Kelly looked as if
steam might come out of her ears at any
moment. 'Right. Help me pick up this
washing and bring it into the house. It
will all have to be done again. I have to
go down the lane to Buttercup Farm, so

since you're the one who made the sheets
all muddy, *you're* going to be the one to
wash them!'

For some reason, Mrs Kelly hadn't
mentioned Arrow. It was almost as if she
couldn't see him.

'Me! Do washing? But I've never –'
Becky began and then stopped as Mrs
Kelly gave her a stern look. 'OK then.
Will you show me how the washing
machine works?'

'That's better. Follow me.'

The moment the housekeeper's back
was turned, Becky quickly hid Arrow
under her T-shirt. She sighed. This was
terrible. The last thing she'd expected
to be doing on the first day of her farm
holiday was washing sheets!

Chapter
FOUR

Becky sat cross-legged on the utility room floor, where she'd been for the past ten minutes, staring glumly at the washing machine. Mrs Kelly had gone out, after giving Becky strict orders not to move a muscle until all the sheets were done.

'That woman is super-scary. I bet she'll snitch on me to Uncle Den and insist that he grounds me! And how come she didn't

seem to notice I was holding you?' she
asked Arrow, who sat in her lap, calmly
grooming himself.

The magic bunny looked up at Becky,
the tip of his little pink tongue still
sticking out.

'I used my magic, so that only you can
see and hear me.'

'You can make yourself invisible?
Cool!' Becky smiled, wondering what
else her magical friend could do. 'I wish
that could help us do the washing. These
sheets are taking a long time. I reckon we
could be here for ages.'

Arrow put his head on one side. 'I do
not think so.'

Becky felt the familiar prickling
sensation down her back as Arrow's
magic key began pulsing again with a

glowing light. Another cloud of sparkling
crystal dust appeared and trickled
down onto the washing machine. The
machine started whizzing round at
super-fast speed. Becky's eyes widened
in amazement as it stopped dead with a
loud burping noise. The door flew open

and out came the clean sheets, floating through the air like ghosts and drifting out of the back door.

Becky scrambled to her feet and ran after them. She was just in time to see the sheets drape themselves magically over the washing line.

Snap! Snap! Snap! A row of unused clothespegs, dangling from the line, marched towards the sheets like a line of soldiers and clipped themselves smartly into place.

Becky clapped her hands in delight. 'That was fantastic! Thanks, Arrow. That would have been a horrible job. Let's go upstairs now and I can show you my bedroom.'

*

Becky and Arrow had just reached the landing when Leon's bedroom door opened.

'What was all that shouting downstairs earlier?' he asked curiously.

Becky stiffened and started to hide Arrow behind her back before she remembered that he was invisible.

'That was Mrs Kelly. She had a major stress at me!' she told him, rolling her eyes.

'Why?' Leon asked.

Becky told him about tripping over into the sheets, being careful not to mention anything about Arrow. She was halfway through explaining when Leon began grinning and then laughing out loud.

'I wish I'd seen her face when she saw you trampling her clean washing! You're a lot braver than I am!'

Becky looked at him in astonishment. Someone seemed to have stolen her quiet, serious cousin and put this boy with the infectious laugh in his place. She found herself smiling with him and then both of them fell about laughing.

'Killer Kelly was so angry! I thought her apron was going to ping right off, like

the clothespegs!' she gasped, dabbing at
her eyes with her T-shirt.

'Killer Kelly? That really suits her!'
Leon laughed, holding his ribs.

Arrow watched them both from
Becky's arms, with a look of puzzlement
in his big soft brown eyes. He shook his
head slowly.

'Humans are very strange sometimes.'

Becky laughed even more. 'Arr– um . . .
I mean . . . *Anyway,*' she quickly corrected
herself. She would have to be a lot more
careful about keeping Arrow a secret.
'I've done the sheets in double-quick
time. I was just going up to my room, cos
I didn't fancy being around when Mrs
Kelly gets back.'

'I don't blame you.' Leon looked
thoughtful. 'Come on!' he said, edging

past her and starting to walk downstairs.

'Where are we going?'

'Somewhere I often go. Somewhere secret,' he said mysteriously.

Becky was intrigued by the fact that her cousin was including her in something for the first time ever. She didn't need telling twice. 'You're on!'

Arrow nudged Becky gently, obviously as eager as she was about having an adventure. She tucked him more securely under her arm before hurrying after Leon. It wasn't a moment too soon. As Becky, Arrow and Leon crossed the kitchen, they heard the front door opening.

'Hello, Becky,' Mrs Kelly called. 'How's that washing doing?'

'Leg it!' Becky whispered.

Leon shot out of the kitchen door and

headed down the garden. Becky raced after him, but slowed down when she saw the tall, prickly hawthorn hedge that formed a barrier at the bottom.

'It's a dead end!'

'No, it's not! This way!' Leon kneeled down and wriggled through a gap near the ground that Becky hadn't noticed.

She put Arrow down so he could hop through and then picked him up again after she emerged. 'Are you OK?' she whispered.

'I am fine.' He settled in her arms again.

Leon looked back at her and frowned. Becky realized he had heard her.

'Just talking to myself. It's a habit of mine!' she said, scrambling upright.

They jogged down a narrow strip of grass that ran along the edge of a cornfield. Leon was ahead of her and just turning on to a rough track.

Becky ran after him. This was fun – like doing cross-country at school!

After a couple of minutes, Leon paused. 'That's where we're going,' he said, pointing to a hill that rose above the farm.

Becky shaded her eyes to look at it. It was mainly grass with just a few scrubby bushes on the slopes.

'What's so special about it?' she whispered to Arrow, as Leon quickened his pace again. 'Maybe there are really good views from the top or something.'

Arrow nodded.

Tall heads of corn rustled in the warm breeze and skylarks called overhead as they jogged onwards. Becky could see the woods she'd glimpsed from her bedroom window and the towering shapes of other hills much further away.

She'd almost caught up with Leon now. Putting on a spurt, she drew level and then ran past him, her trainers pounding the ground.

'Last one to the top is a muppet!' she cried.

'No, wait!' Leon cried.

But Becky took no notice as she sped away. 'Eat my dust!' she crowed.

Holding Arrow didn't slow her down. Even cradling him carefully, Becky was a fast runner. They reached the hilltop seconds ahead of Leon.

'Yay!' she cried triumphantly.

Panting, Leon pushed back a strand of damp blond hair as he caught up with her. 'Are you always like this?'

'Pretty much!' Becky said, grinning.
She bent her knees to let Arrow jump
down and flopped onto the grass while
he hopped over to a patch of clover.

'I was *trying* to tell you that we have
to be quiet up here if we want to see
anything,' Leon told her, sounding a bit
miffed. 'The wild rabbits that live here are
quite used to me, but you're a stranger so

they might take longer to come out.'

'Oh, sorry.' Becky smiled sheepishly.
She did get carried away sometimes. She
turned over onto her tummy to watch
Arrow nibbling the juicy leaves. *Even if
the wild rabbits are feeling shy, I can see one
special bunny right now!*

Just then Arrow's ears twitched and
his big brown eyes glowed with tiny
rainbows as he looked more closely at the
hilltop. 'There is a warren here. Like back
home in Moonglow Meadow!'

He gave a mighty leap, followed by
three hops and disappeared down the
nearest burrow.

Chapter
FIVE

'Arrow!' Becky gasped in shock, only just managing not to leap straight to her feet and take off after him.

Why had he run away? She hoped the magic bunny hadn't decided that he'd rather hide among his wild cousins.

'Why did you say "arrow"?' Leon asked, looking at Becky curiously.

'Oh, well . . . erm . . .' Becky didn't

know quite how to answer without
giving away the little magic bunny.
But luckily, just then, Leon forgot their
conversation.

'Look!' He grabbed Becky's arm and
pointed towards a large greyish-coloured
rabbit emerging from a burrow a couple
of metres away. Its nose twitched as it
stood up on its back legs, watchful and
alert. 'That's Smudge – at least that's what
I call her because of that brown mark on
her right ear. She's the top female.'

'Smudge?' Becky echoed, too worried about Arrow to concentrate properly.

She hesitated, trying to decide what to do. Her instincts told her to go closer to the warren and check out some of the burrows for any sign of her friend. But how could she explain that to Leon without giving Arrow away? She'd come really close already.

Becky forced herself to calm down. As hard as it was to wait, she would have to trust Arrow.

Leon was watching as other rabbits emerged. Soon, more adults stood up on their legs all around the warren, sniffing the air for possible enemies. Then, at some kind of invisible signal, six of the tiniest rabbits Becky had ever seen appeared from a burrow right beside Smudge.

'Look at those. Aren't they sweet?' Leon turned towards her to whisper. 'Baby rabbits are called kits. This is the first time I've seen them out of their burrows. Smudge has been feeding them on milk in a special underground chamber, until they're old enough to eat grass.'

Becky's heart melted. They were very cute.

Suddenly, she spotted a familiar tiny fluffy pale-coffee-coloured shape hopping towards Smudge. Arrow!

'There he is!' Becky exclaimed. 'I mean . . . there they are,' she quickly corrected herself, pointing at the kits.

Becky watched closely as Arrow stopped in front of Smudge. The tiny magic bunny looked about half the size of the lead female. Smudge laid her ears flat and her eyes rolled as she reared up above him with her front paws outstretched.

Smudge was going to attack Arrow!

Becky caught her breath, worried that her friend would be hurt. But the wild rabbit eventually sank back down and crouched head to head with Arrow. The two rabbits stayed motionless for a few seconds before Arrow touched his pink nose to the wild rabbit's muzzle. Smudge bowed her head as if in farewell.

To Becky's relief, she saw the magic bunny give a flick of his tail as he

hopped away from the warren and came bounding back towards her. Becky felt her tension easing as the little rabbit settled down with his warm furry body pressed against her bare arm. Leon was busy looking at the kits, so Becky risked talking to Arrow.

'When you ran off like that, I thought you'd gone to live with the wild rabbits and didn't want to be my friend any more,' she whispered.

Arrow's floppy little ears drooped. 'I am sorry. I should have explained that I was only exploring. I am very happy with you, Becky.'

'That's OK then.' Becky stroked his fluffy fur, feeling a bit silly now for being so worried. 'Because I love having you for my friend!'

They settled down together to watch
the wild rabbits. Becky was able to
concentrate properly now. She noticed
quite a lot of difference in the colours of
their fur. Some of the rabbits were quite
a dark brown and others were almost grey.

Leon edged closer on his tummy and
started scribbling in a notebook as he
studied another group of larger rabbits
that Becky assumed were males. She was
really enjoying being here with him.
Maybe being quiet sometimes wasn't so
bad after all.

'The lead female is a fine rabbit,' Arrow
told her.

'Leon calls her Smudge,' Becky whispered
back. 'Because of the mark on her ear.'

Arrow nodded approval. 'Smudge. That
is a good name.'

All at once, Becky noticed that the key
round Arrow's neck was shining brightly.

Arrow saw her looking. 'Moonglow
Meadow will soon be in need of more of
the key's magic,' he explained.

'Do you have to leave?' Becky
whispered anxiously.

Arrow looked up at her with serious
eyes. 'Not yet. But if the key glows
constantly, I might have to leave suddenly,
without saying goodbye.'

'But you can come back here again
afterwards, can't you?'

Arrow shook his head. 'I am afraid that is

not possible, Becky. Once I leave here, the magic trail to this place is closed forever. I hope you understand,' he said gently.

Becky pressed her lips together as she nodded, hoping like mad that this wouldn't happen too soon. She had barely recovered from the fright Arrow had given her when he had wandered off, and she wanted to enjoy every single moment she could with him.

Sitting back in the warm sunshine, Becky, Arrow and Leon watched the wild rabbits all around them. The creatures fed and groomed themselves, perfectly at ease.

Leon gave a muffled cry of delight as some of the kits leapt high in the air and kicked out with their tiny back legs so that they changed direction.

'Did you see that? Rabbits do that
twisting jumping thing when they're
happy. It's called a binky.'

Becky felt her interest quickening. She
hadn't seen Arrow do a binky. Maybe
magic bunnies showed they were happy
in other ways. 'How come you know all
this stuff?' she asked Leon.

'I've been reading up about wild
rabbits. Most people just take them for
granted, but they're really interesting once
you start looking more closely. We didn't

even *have* rabbits in this country until the Normans brought them here.'

'I didn't know that.' Becky was impressed. There was more to her cousin than she'd realized. 'Is this the kind of stuff you write about for the online 'zine Uncle Den told me about?'

'Yep. And tons of other stuff about animals and insects. I'm going to be a wildlife reporter when I'm older.'

Becky believed him. 'I think you'd be great at it.'

Leon looked pleased but then he frowned. 'I don't think I'll ever convince Dad about rabbits, though. He's always complaining that they're eating his crops and threatening to do something about it.'

'Yes. He mentioned that at breakfast, just after you'd gone upstairs,' Becky said.

'Did he?' Leon asked worriedly. 'I wonder what he has in mind.'

Becky searched her memory. 'He said he was going to "take action" or something like that. Maybe he's going to trap them and then let them free somewhere else?'

'I wish,' Leon said. A serious look flickered across his face. 'There are lots of harsher ways to deal with a rabbit problem. If you ask me, this warren's in real danger.'

Chapter
SIX

It was late afternoon as Becky, Arrow
and Leon made their way back to the
farmhouse. Leon was lagging behind, deep
in thought. Becky knew he was worrying
about the wild rabbits, as she was.

Arrow lay in the curve of Becky's arm,
with his fluffy front paws crossed. 'What
did Leon mean about the warren being in
danger?'

Becky wasn't exactly sure, but she had
a fair idea. She hated telling him, but he
would have to find out soon enough.

'Leon thinks Uncle Den is planning
to use ways to . . . um . . . cut down the
numbers of rabbits. Like getting rid of the
warren,' she said gently.

Arrow looked shocked. 'That is
terrible!'

Becky nodded, feeling awful. 'Yes,
I know.' She couldn't bear to think of

anything bad happening to the wild
rabbits, especially Smudge and her kits.

'There must be something we can
do!' Arrow said, his whiskers twitching
anxiously.

Becky racked her brains to come up
with a solution as they reached the gap
in the hawthorn hedge. She had a sudden
flare of hope as she remembered how
Arrow and Smudge had stood head to
head, as if they might be communicating.

'Can magic bunnies talk to wild
rabbits?'

'No. We are only distantly related to
them. They do not speak our language.
But Smudge is a very intelligent rabbit.
I could sense some of her thoughts in
pictures.'

Becky hid her disappointment.

'I thought you might be able to warn her about the danger, so she could tell the rabbits to stop eating the crops.'

'I do not think that can happen. Did you notice how the plants around the hill have been nibbled right down?' Arrow asked sadly. 'The warren is large. I think there are too many hungry rabbits here.'

Becky had a flash of inspiration. 'I know! You could use the magic key to make the hill green and lush again – like Moonglow Meadow!'

Arrow nodded slowly. 'It might work for a little while. But I will not always be here when the hill needs more magic. And the rabbits will be too hungry to resist eating your uncle's corn and cabbages again.'

Becky realized she had to face facts.

A solution didn't look very likely.

Supper was a delicious lasagne and salad, made by Mrs Kelly, who had already left to go home, much to Becky and Leon's relief.

Becky was sure the housekeeper must have told Uncle Den about the washing incident. She waited expectantly for him to mention it, but nothing happened.

After supper was cleared away, they all trooped into the sitting room. Leon wanted to watch a wildlife documentary about bats. Becky was quite looking forward to it too. She'd just curled up with Arrow on her lap when her uncle spoke. 'Mrs Kelly had a word with me earlier . . .'

Becky held her breath. She steeled

herself for a serious telling-off.

'. . . about the chicken feed,' her uncle
went on. 'She noticed we were getting
low on supplies. Could you order some
more for me online, Leon?'

'Yep. No probs. I'll go and do it after
this TV programme.'

Becky couldn't believe it. 'Mrs Kelly
didn't snitch on me!' she whispered to
Arrow. 'Maybe she isn't that bad after all.'

Arrow was curling up into a furry ball.

'I am glad you did not get into trouble,' he said sleepily.

Becky smiled down at him. It had been a long day for a tiny bunny. 'You have a nice nap,' she whispered, gently cuddling him. She noticed Leon looking across at her and wondered if he'd noticed anything strange. Surely he couldn't see Arrow, who was still invisible?

But Leon gave Becky a shy smile. 'You seemed to have a good time today. So I wondered if you'd like to have a look at some of my wildlife stuff?'

'Yeah, I'd love to!' Becky said eagerly.

'Great! You can read the bits I've written for the 'zine too, if you like.'

'Don't push it!' Becky joked, rolling her eyes.

Leon laughed.

As she settled down to watch TV,
Becky felt pleased that she and her cousin
were getting on a bit better. She thought
she'd definitely made the right decision to
stay at the farmhouse. If only they could
think of some way to help Smudge and
the other rabbits, everything would be
great.

The following day it rained. Becky stared
glumly out of the farmhouse window
at the deep puddles and muddy ruts in
the yard. She had been hoping that they
would go to check on the warren, but the
rain showed no sign of stopping.

'Oh well. I suppose we're staying inside
today,' she sighed. 'Maybe I could read
one of Leon's wildlife books. He's got
tons of them in his bedroom.'

Arrow sat beside Becky on the window
sill as she looked through one of Leon's
books. He lifted a fluffy front paw to bat at
the raindrops trickling down the pane outside.

Becky laughed. Her friend's cute antics
could always cheer her up.

'At least the rabbits will be safe. No
one's going to do anything about them
in this downpour,' she said, giving him
a cuddle.

Becky had thought Leon might shut himself away with his computer, but instead he appeared in the sitting room with a big pad of brightly coloured paper. 'Ever done origami?' he asked.

'Nope,' Becky admitted. 'But I'll have a go!'

Becky soon found out she was pretty good at folding paper into animal shapes. Before long, she was admiring the line of paper animals marching along the coffee table, even if some of them had wonky legs.

Leon was brilliant at origami. He even made an amazing T. rex.

The day passed surprisingly quickly. Delicious smells from the kitchen filled the whole house, making Becky's mouth water. Mrs Kelly popped her head round the door to say there were cheese scones and chocolate cake for tea.

'And I've brought you some of my home-made ginger beer.'

'Wow! What a feast. Can we have it in here on a tray, for a special treat?' Leon asked.

The housekeeper put her hands on her hips. 'What, and get crumbs everywhere?

I should think not. Come along and sit at the kitchen table.'

Becky and Leon exchanged looks, but did as they were told. As she ate, Becky crumbled up bits of scone and dropped them under the table. Arrow hopped about eagerly snuffling them all up. She was glad he was invisible or house-proud Mrs Kelly would have had a fit!

'This cake is yummy! Chocolate cream *and* icing with whopping great chocolate drops on top!' Leon said. 'Killer Kelly might be a pain, but she's an amazing cook!'

After they had finished, Becky, Arrow and Leon went back to the sitting room.

'What shall we do now?' Becky asked, hoping her cousin had some more good ideas.

'I dunno,' Leon murmured. His mood seemed to have suddenly changed. 'I can't stop thinking about the rabbits, especially Smudge and her kits.'

Becky was worried too, but she always tried to look on the bright side. 'You never know. Something might happen to save them.'

'Yeah? And pigs might fly!'

Leon looked so troubled that Becky wondered what she could do to cheer him up.

She remembered the stuff she'd read about in the wildlife books. Maybe talking about his favourite subject might take his mind off it – even for just a little while. It was worth a try.

Without really thinking it through, Becky began in a rush. 'I never knew

that only female rabbits dig burrows. Or
that they don't hibernate. And their teeth
keep on growing forever . . .' she said,
enthusiastically listing more facts. She
paused for breath and saw Leon glaring at
her. 'What?'

'The warren's in danger and you don't
even care! All you can do is babble on
and on, like you're giving a speech or
something!'

'I do care!' Becky protested, shocked. 'I
just thought –'

'Just leave it,' Leon muttered. 'I wish I'd

never taken you to see the warren.' He jumped up and left the room.

Becky looked at Arrow in dismay. 'Do you think he meant that?' She was ready to go straight after Leon. 'I'm going to ask him!'

Arrow laid a tiny soft paw on her arm. 'I think Leon needs to be alone.'

Becky felt herself calming down as she looked at her wise little friend. Reaching out, she stroked his warm soft ears. 'I guess you're right. I s'pose I did go on a bit. I just hope that things go back to how they were before. We'd been getting on so well.'

Chapter
SEVEN

The following day dawned bright and clear.
Becky's uncle had planned to drive into
the nearest village to take his car to a garage.

Leon followed his dad out into the yard.

Becky hung back a bit. Leon had
been quiet at breakfast and they had
only exchanged a word or two. She felt
awkward with him since their argument.

'Can Becky and I come with you?' she

heard Leon ask.

Becky looked up in surprise.

'I could be an hour or two with the mechanic,' his dad replied. 'Won't you two be bored?'

'Nah. We can go to the library and then I'll show Becky round the village.' Leon glanced at her over his shoulder and gave an apologetic grin. 'Are you coming or what?'

'You bet!' Becky jumped at the chance of an outing, especially as Mrs Kelly had just declared that she was going to spring-clean the downstairs rooms.

Her uncle smiled. 'Come on then, you two.'

'I'll just pop upstairs and grab my bag,' Becky said.

Becky found Arrow sitting on her

duvet, grooming himself. 'Yay! Leon's fine with me now and we're all going into the village. Do you want to get into my bag? You'll be safer in there.'

Arrow nodded eagerly.

Uncle Den started the motor and then pulled out on to the farm track. Becky sat in the back of the car with her bag on the seat beside her, so Arrow could peer out at the countryside.

Sunshine poured down on a patchwork of fields and the green hills in the distance. Becky saw sheep on hillsides and herds of black-and-white cows. Now and then she saw a rabbit feeding on a grass verge and felt a new pang of concern for the warren above Foxglove Farm.

Uncle Den dropped them at the library, and after spending time looking around

at the books, they wandered through
the village. Arrow peered out of the bag
and his nose twitched at the interesting
smells. Becky smiled to see him enjoying
himself. The three of them passed by a
cottage that had a fancy iron gate topped
by a handsome iron rabbit.

A shaft of sunlight caught the gate and
threw a large dark rabbit-shaped shadow
on to the pavement right in front of
Arrow.

The magic bunny's eyes rolled in fright. 'My enemies have found me!' Leaping out of the bag, he landed on the pavement and shot down the street like a rocket.

'Oh no!' Becky gasped.

Without a second thought, she hurtled down the street after her tiny friend, who was already far ahead of her. Becky just glimpsed his bobtail flashing as he disappeared round a corner.

'Hey! Where are you going? Wait for me!' Leon cried behind her.

Becky didn't look round. Her heart was in her mouth. She felt frantic at the thought of the dangers of traffic and people who might accidentally trip over her invisible friend.

Rounding the corner, she glimpsed the

village green ahead. There was an ancient-looking tree in the centre. A wooden bench stood beneath it. Becky spotted a familiar little figure cowering underneath it.

'Arrow!' she gasped, weak with relief.

She ran over to him, threw herself on to the grass and reached under the bench. 'You're safe now,' she crooned. Holding his trembling little form, she explained about how the shadow rabbit had appeared.

She could feel Arrow's tiny heart beating fast as she sank onto the bench with him and gently stroked his fluffy pale-coffee-coloured fur.

'I am sorry, I panicked. Thank you for coming to find me.'

'I'm just glad you're OK,' Becky said fondly. She didn't know what she'd do if anything happened to her magical friend.

Leon ran across the green towards Becky and Arrow. 'There you are!' he puffed. 'Why did you run off like that?'

Becky thought fast. 'It was a game of tag. First one to the tree. And I won!' she improvized madly.

He looked puzzled. 'So how come you didn't tell me it was a race?'

Becky shrugged. 'It was more fun this way.'

'You're weird!' Leon shook his head slowly.

'That makes two of us!' she replied spiritedly.

Leon pretended to look offended. Then he grinned and plonked himself onto the bench beside her. 'Fair enough. Maybe that's why we get on.'

They both started laughing. Becky was delighted to hear her cousin thought they were getting on too.

Becky relaxed, enjoying the shade under the old tree. She wondered what Leon would say if he knew that there was an invisible magic bunny so close to him.

She glanced idly towards some shops opposite the green and saw her uncle coming out of one of them. 'Look, there's Uncle Den . . .' she began, and then her heart sank as she noticed the sign above the door that read *A & R. Wilson. Pest Control Specialists.*

'Oh no!' she groaned. Her uncle had decided to take drastic action to protect his crops.

Chapter
EIGHT

That evening, Becky was going downstairs
with Arrow when she heard raised voices
coming from inside the kitchen.

'So what's wrong with rabbit-proof
fences?' Leon demanded.

'I've already told you. They're just
not practical on a farm this size,' his dad
replied patiently. 'We use a lot of big
machinery and need easy access to the

fields. Not to mention the huge cost of new fencing. It's the same with trapping and moving the rabbits. It would just take too long and in the meantime more crops would be lost.'

'But what you're planning to do . . . it's horrible!' Leon sounded close to tears.

'I don't like this situation either. But I have to do what's best for the farm. You're a farmer's son, Leon, and you must learn to be realistic.' Becky thought Uncle Den sounded weary, as if he was tired of arguing. 'The pest control people will be here tomorrow. They'll do a good job. No rabbits will suffer.'

'I won't let you do this!' Leon yelled. 'There's got to be some other way –'

'That's enough!' his dad replied. 'I don't want to hear another word.'

Leon stormed out of the kitchen and ran upstairs past Becky. She heard the kitchen door slam behind her uncle.

Becky sighed and her shoulders drooped. 'Did you hear that? We've only got until tomorrow to think of a way to make Uncle Den change his mind.'

Arrow nodded sadly. His dewy brown eyes, with their rainbow twinkles, looked troubled.

They went into the garden so Arrow could eat some grass. As Becky sat watching him, she found herself looking towards the hills beyond the woods.

Something about those steep green slopes got her thinking.

'There must be tons of grass on those hills and they're miles away from anywhere,' she said. 'Why can't the rabbits go and live there, where no one would bother them?'

Arrow pricked up his ears. 'It is a good idea, Becky. But it could take a long time to persuade Smudge and the others to leave their home. They would want to explore the new place first by sending out scouts and then move gradually if all was well.'

Becky bit her lip as she thought of the difficulty of persuading hundreds of rabbits to move in just a few short hours. It seemed almost impossible, but she wasn't prepared to give up yet.

The germ of an idea started to form.

'I know magic bunnies can't talk to wild rabbits,' she said to Arrow. 'But you said you could sense Smudge's thoughts in pictures, didn't you?

Arrow nodded. 'That is right.'

'So – if you needed to tell her something really important, you could imagine it in pictures and she'd be able to understand you?' Becky asked.

'I do not know. But I could try.'

'Right. This is what I think we should do,' Becky warmed to her idea. 'We wait until everyone's asleep tonight, then we go to the warren and . . .'

As she finished explaining, Arrow's whiskers twitched excitedly. 'It is a good plan!'

*

Later that evening, Arrow was curled up on Becky's duvet. Outside the window, a glorious sunset had spread flame colours across the darkening sky.

'I'm just going to pop downstairs to tell Uncle Den and Leon that I'm having an early night,' Becky said. 'I don't want anyone coming in later and seeing I'm gone.'

She found Uncle Den and Leon in the sitting room. Leon was sitting hunched in a chair with his arms folded. He looked a picture of misery as he thought about what was to happen the following morning. Becky wished she could tell him what she and Arrow planned to do, but it had to remain a secret.

'Goodnight, love. Sleep tight,' her uncle said.

Back upstairs, Becky got into bed with
her clothes on and lay there cuddling
Arrow. She was sure that she was far too
excited to sleep.

But she must have dropped off, because
it seemed like only moments later when
she felt Arrow nudging her cheek
urgently with his damp nose.

'Wake up. We must go!'

Chapter
NINE

Bright moonlight flooded the garden.
Becky peered out of the kitchen door
with Arrow by her feet as she got ready
to run towards the gap in the hedge. But
then suddenly she felt a familiar warm
prickle down her spine as Arrow's key
flashed and a big whoosh of crystal dust
swirled around her like a small tornado
and instantly transported them both to

the top of the hill.

'Whoa!' Becky steadied herself after the amazing journey. She loved magic! She checked to see that Arrow was OK too and noticed that the little bunny's key was still flashing. Before she could wonder why, Becky felt a light and fizzy whoosh run through her – just like bubbling lemonade – and she looked down to see her own feet had turned into greyish-brown paws!

Paws? Next to her, Arrow seemed to have grown in size. Oh, wow! She was a wild rabbit!

'Cool!' Becky blinked in amazement. Everything looked extra bright and clear through her large rabbit eyes.

'This way,' Arrow told her, hopping towards the warren. 'We must find Smudge.'

As Becky moved forward, she immediately tripped over in a messy tangle of legs and paws. It wasn't very easy with four feet! Taking a deep breath, she tried again. This time she managed a rather wobbly hop, but the next one was better and she soon got the hang of it.

'Wait for me!' she called, chasing after Arrow.

As they got closer to the warren, they saw dozens of rabbits hopping about above ground. Some were feeding, while others kept watch. Becky spotted a large grey-brown rabbit with six kits in tow.

'Smudge!'

Arrow had seen the lead female too. He hopped towards her and Smudge reared up on to her back legs in welcome.

Becky watched anxiously as Arrow and Smudge stood with their heads close together, just as they'd done on that first visit with Leon. Would Arrow be able to make Smudge understand that the whole warren was in great danger and that they must all move quickly?

Arrow came back towards Becky.

'How did it go?' she asked.

He hunched his furry shoulders. 'She understood, but she is anxious. The hills seem very far away and she does not know if the land there is suitable to make a new warren.'

'But it looks perfect!' Becky said.

Arrow nodded. 'I think so too. That is why I have promised Smudge that you and I are going to lead them there.'

'We are?' Becky gulped worriedly. But she trusted her magical friend. 'Um . . . OK then.'

She felt the ground vibrate beneath her paws as first Smudge and then dozens of other rabbits thumped their feet. It was the signal for them to leave. More rabbits poured out of the burrows, some of them holding kits gently in their mouths.

And then, headed by Smudge, they hopped towards Arrow and Becky.

'Ready?' Arrow flashed Becky a reassuring glance from chocolate-brown eyes that gleamed with rainbow light.

Becky nodded. As her friend sprang forward, she leapt with him. They kept pace, side by side, as they hopped down the hill and past fields of crops.

Hundreds of rabbits formed a grey-brown stream that seemed to pour after them as they left Foxglove Farm behind. They passed through fields, down paths

and across quiet empty roads. When
they reached the woods Arrow sped on,
confidently weaving through the trees.

Becky's legs were starting to feel tired
by the time they led Smudge and the
other rabbits up the slopes of the once-
distant hills. At long last Arrow stopped,
his sides heaving, and Becky paused
beside him.

Smudge hopped over to Arrow. She

dipped her head as if to thank him and then snuffled around for a few seconds before scrabbling at the soil with her strong paws. Other rabbits came forward and did the same.

'They're building new burrows!' Becky exclaimed delightedly.

Arrow flicked his tail with satisfaction. 'Yes, Becky. Our work here is done.'

Becky felt a warm sense of pride as she looked at all the rabbits working hard to make a new warren. They would be safe here.

But before she could say anything else, she saw Arrow's key flashing again and another cloud of crystal dust surrounded them both.

There was a whooshing sensation and a blur of speed. Becky felt herself landing

gently on her behind. She felt soft grass
against her hands as she got up. *Hands!*
She was a girl again.

She looked around for Arrow and saw
him nearby. They were back at the old
warren on the hill above Foxglove Farm.
It was getting light and the first rays of
sunlight gleamed on Arrow's pale fur.
Suddenly he leapt into the air, kicked out
his back legs and changed direction.

'Hey! You did a *binky*!' Becky said.

'Yes. I am happy because we saved
the rabbits!'

'We did, didn't we?' Becky said,
beaming at him. 'We're a great team!'

A strange look of happiness mixed with
sadness spread across Arrow's face.

Becky saw that his key was glowing
brightly, as if it had the sun inside it. The

moment she had been dreading was here.
More shimmering crystal dust appeared,
swirling around Arrow and twinkling
with rainbow sparkles.

Suddenly, he appeared in his true form
– a tiny fluffy pale-coffee-coloured bunny
no longer, but a majestic rabbit the size of
a large cat. His silky pure white fur was
flecked with silver and his large ears had
gleaming silver tips.

'Arrow!' Becky gasped. She had almost
forgotten how glorious he was. 'You . . .
you're leaving right now, aren't you?'

He nodded. Rainbows glimmered in
his big chocolate-brown eyes. 'I must.
Moonglow Meadow urgently needs more
of the key's magic.'

Becky's throat felt tight as she tried to
hold back tears. She knew she must

be brave and not beg him to stay. 'I'll
never forget you,' she whispered brokenly.
Rushing forward, she bent down and
gathered the handsome white rabbit in
her arms.

'You have been a good friend, Becky.
I will never forget you either.' Arrow
allowed her to give him one final cuddle
and then moved away slowly. 'Farewell,

Becky. Remember always to follow your dreams,' he said in a soft voice.

There was a final flash of light, and crystal dust showered down around Becky and tinkled like fairy bells as it hit the ground. Arrow faded and was gone.

Becky gave in to tears – she knew she was going to miss Arrow dreadfully.

Something lay on the grass by her feet. It was a single rainbow crystal drop. Wiping her eyes, Becky bent down and picked it up. The drop fizzed against her palm as it turned into a pure white pebble in the shape of a bunny.

Becky slipped it into her pocket. She would keep it as a reminder of the magic bunny and the wonderful adventure they had shared.

'Becky!'

She looked up to see Leon running towards her.

'I came to have one last look at the rabbits, before . . . you know,' he said, chewing at his lip. 'You weren't in your bedroom, so I guessed you'd be here.' He frowned as he saw she was smiling. 'What?'

'They've all gone!' she said. 'The warren's empty. The rabbits must have left in the night!'

Leon looked puzzled. 'I don't get it.' He went to investigate and then stood looking at the deserted hillside. 'You're right. It even feels different. I don't know what happened, but it's brilliant! I hope Smudge and the others have gone far away.'

'They have,' Becky assured him. 'I mean

. . . I've got a hunch that they've found somewhere even better to live.'

'Me too!' Leon beamed at her. 'Maybe we could go and look for them? We've got the rest of the week.'

'Fine by me!' Becky said happily. She felt proud of what she and Arrow had achieved, even though she could never tell anyone about it.

I hope you get home safely. Take care of Moonglow Meadow, Arrow, she whispered under her breath.

Out Now

Magic Bunny

Out Now

Could you be this tiny bunny's special friend?

Magic Bunny

Dancing Days

SUE BENTLEY

Look Out For

Magic Bunny

Chocolate Wishes
9780141332413

Holiday Dreams
9780141332420

Dancing Days
9780141332437

Classroom Capers
9780141332444

A Splash of Magic
9780141332451

Magic Ponies

A New Friend
9780141325934

A Special Wish
9780141325941

A Twinkle of Hooves
9780141325958

Showjumping Dreams
9780141325965

Seaside Summer
9780141325972

Riding Rescue
9780141325989

Winter Wonderland
9780141327723

Pony Camp
9780141327730

A Christmas Wish
9780141325996

puffin.co.uk

Magic Puppy

A New Beginning
9780141323503

Muddy Paws
9780141323510

Cloud Capers
9780141323527

Star of the Show
9780141323534

Party Dreams
9780141323794

A Forest Charm
9780141323800

Twirling Tails
9780141323817

School of Mischief
9780141323824

Snowy Wishes
9780141323831

Classroom Princess
9780141324791

Friendship Forever
9780141324784

Sparkling Skates
9780141324777

Sunshine Shimmers
9780141324760

Spellbound at School

The Perfect Secret
9780141324746

A little puppy,
a sprinkling of magic,
a forever friend

If you like
Magic Puppy,
you'll love

A Summer Spell
9780141320144

Classroom Chaos
9780141320151

Star Dreams
9780141320168

Double Trouble
9780141320175

Moonlight Mischief
9780141321530

A Circus Wish
9780141321547

Sparkling Steps
9780141321554

A Glittering Gallop
9780141321561

Seaside Mystery
9780141321981

Firelight Friends
9780141321998

A Shimmering Splash
9780141322001

A Puzzle of Paws
9780141322018

A Christmas Surprise
9780141323237

Picture Perfect
9780141323480

A Splash of Forever
9780141323497

Win a Magic Bunny goody bag!

Strike, the leader of the bunnies of Moonglow Meadow,
has an urgent message for Arrow that will keep him safe from the
dark rabbits who are trying to capture the magic key.

Two words from the message can be found in the special carrots
that are hidden in *Holiday Dreams* and *Dancing Days*. Find the hidden
words and put them together to complete Strike's message.
Send it into us and each month we will put every correct message
in a draw and pick out one lucky winner who will
receive a special Magic Bunny prize.

Send your secret message, name and address on a postcard to:
Magic Bunny competition
Puffin Books
80 Strand
London WC2R 0RL

Hurry, Arrow needs your help!

Good luck!

puffin.co.uk

It all started with a Scarecrow.

Puffin is seventy years old.
Sounds ancient, doesn't it? But Puffin has never been
so lively. We're always on the lookout for the next big
idea, which is how it began all those years ago.

Penguin Books was a big idea from the mind of
a man called Allen Lane, who in 1935 invented
the quality paperback and changed the world.
**And from great Penguins, great Puffins grew,
changing the face of children's books forever.**

The first four Puffin Picture Books were hatched in 1940 and the
first Puffin story book featured a man with broomstick arms called
Worzel Gummidge. In 1967 Kaye Webb, Puffin Editor, started the
Puffin Club, promising to **'make children into readers'**.
She kept that promise and over 200,000 children became
devoted Puffineers through their quarterly instalments of
Puffin Post, which is now back for a new generation.

Many years from now, we hope you'll look back and
remember Puffin with a smile. **No matter what your age
or what you're into, there's a Puffin for everyone.**
The possibilities are endless, but one thing is for sure:
whether it's a picture book or a paperback, a sticker book
or a hardback, **if it's got that little Puffin
on it – it's bound to be good.**